MADELIA

by Jan Spivey Gilchrist

Dial Books for Young Readers New York

Published by Dial Books for Young Readers
A Division of Penguin Books USA Inc.
375 Hudson Street
New York, New York 10014

Typography by Amelia Lau Carling
Printed in Hong Kong
First Edition
1 3 5 7 9 10 8 6 4 2

Library of Congress Cataloging in Publication Data
Gilchrist, Jan Spivey.
Madelia / by Jan Spivey Gilchrist.
p. cm.
Summary: Madelia would rather be painting with her new
watercolors than going to church,
but as she listens to her father's sermon, she is glad she came.
ISBN 0-8037-2052-1 (trade). — ISBN 0-8037-2054-8 (lib.)
[1. Artists—Fiction. 2. Afro-Americans—Fiction.
3. Church attendance—Fiction. 4. Fathers and daughters—Fiction.]
I. Title. PZ7.G3835Mad 1997 [E]—dc20 96-42266 CIP AC

The full-color art is gouache paintings that were highlighted with pastels.

Special thanks to my models,
Naomi Palacios and Ashley Eiland

For Reverend Charles Spivey (Daddy);
along with food, clothing, and shelter,
you gave me the inspiration to see the world
in all of its beautiful colors.

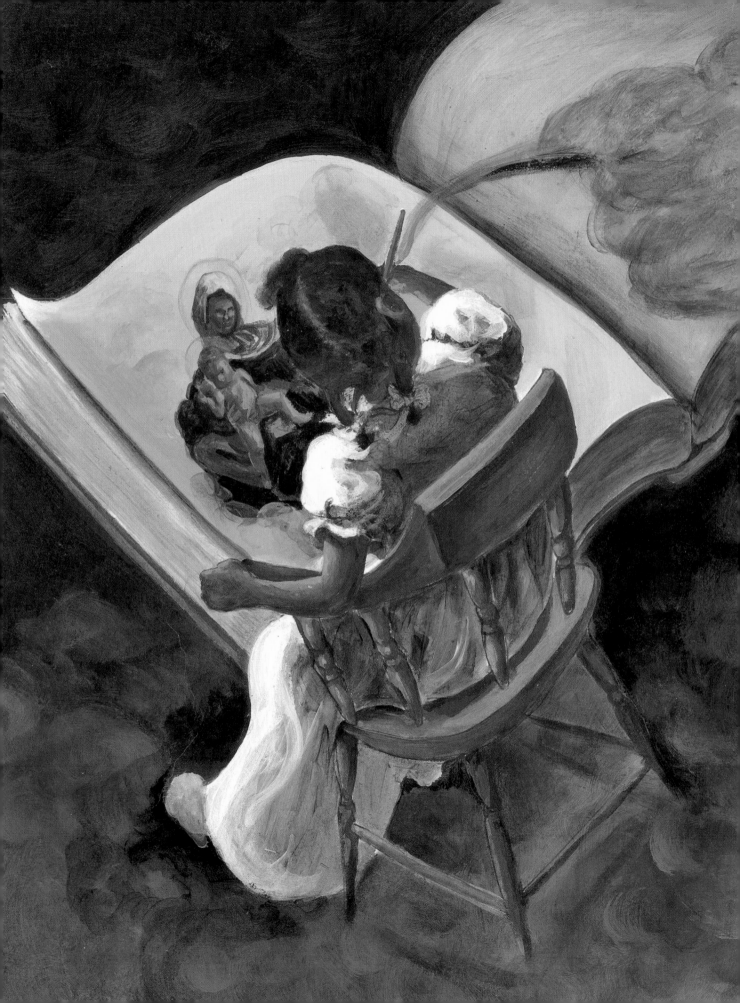

Madelia slept. She dreamed. It was a beautiful dream of bright colors. Visions of her daddy's big Bible filled her head. Stories told in pictures. Stories she knew well and that she didn't need words to tell. She saw herself painting the stories, swirling the paint around on the paper.

"Get up, Madelia," called her mother from the other room. Madelia woke up. Oh, no! It was Sunday! She had to get up and go to church. She had wanted to paint today, with her new watercolors. Six little jars from Aunt Jessie.

Madelia had never had a paint set before, so she only drew black-and-white pictures with her pencils. Now she'd be able to make pictures in colors, pictures that would almost seem to move, just like the ones in the big Bible. Madelia wanted to hurry up and paint, but she had to go to church.

Her mother came into the room. "Madelia," she said, "Junior's out of the bathroom. Go on in there so Melbee can get in next." She placed Madelia's white dress on the table.

Madelia looked at the jars of paints on her dresser. She angrily kicked the covers to the end of the bed. Her chest felt full, and she wanted to scream, "I'm not going to church! I have to paint today!" But she got up and went into the bathroom.

Her feet felt cold on the bathroom floor. The toothpaste wouldn't squirt right. And Junior had dropped her washcloth on the floor. Everything was wrong. It was a terrible Sunday morning.

At breakfast Madelia slouched in her chair and didn't eat. And her sisters and brothers were laughing and talking more than eating.

"Hurry up, you all," her mother said, "so your daddy can get to church early. He's going to preach a new sermon today."

Madelia's daddy frowned. "Delia, sit up and eat," he said, "so we can go. Don't you want to go to church today?"

"Yes, Daddy, but . . ." She didn't want to hurt his feelings. "But, Daddy, I want to paint. I can paint all of those pictures in your Bible now."

Daddy leaned back and looked at Madelia with a look she always saw when he wanted to say something she'd understand later. Then he said mildly, "Well, Delia, you come on to church, and one day you'll paint your own Bible."

Madelia knew that she had to go.

When they reached the church, Sister Banks helped Madelia and her sisters and brothers line up to walk to their seats in the front row. Madelia was first in line, right behind Mama. But as they walked down the aisle, she kept moving back, so she wouldn't have to sit next to Mama. Just because she had to come to church didn't mean she had to sit up straight. She took the seat on the end.

Church began. Brother Hendricks spoke. He talked and talked. Sister Bell talked a little. The choir sang "Didn't It Rain, Children." And then it was time for Daddy. Madelia hoped he wouldn't talk long. Church services could go quickly or they could take hours. Sometimes Daddy's sermons seemed to last forever.

Daddy's voice began slowly. Clearly. Each word sep-
arately. Madelia paid no attention to what the words
meant. She didn't want to hear them. She wanted her
daddy to finish so she could go home and paint.

She slid down in her seat until her feet touched the
floor. Her patent leather shoes shone brightly under
the lights. She let her feet play a game on the floor,
hitting them softly together and putting one on top
of the other.

Her daddy's voice grew louder. It began to have a beat. Madelia tapped her feet to the beat. He spoke, she tapped. Somebody in the congregation answered.

Madelia looked up. Her daddy was walking back and forth. His robe was swinging, moving with the beat. He began to sing his words.

He sang, "Fahh-ther . . . I am your child."

Brother Rivers sang back, "Go 'head, Preacher!"
He struck a chord on the piano. It echoed the words.
Now Madelia's daddy was stepping with the beat.
He spoke with the beat. The congregation echoed.
Madelia tapped.

Suddenly her daddy turned. He moved to Madelia's side of the church. She wondered, Was it her day? Was Daddy going to pick her today? She had never been the special one.

Her daddy stopped in front of her. He knelt down on one knee, his handkerchief in his hand. His shoulders shook from side to side as he wiped his brow.

"Deee - lia!" Daddy sang. His voice started up high and came down. "I say Deee - lia!"

Madelia sat up now and really listened. She looked into his face.

"There is a place . . . a place," Daddy sang out, "oh, yeah . . . a place far away . . . a beautiful place . . . yes, Lord . . . where the streets glisten in the sunlight . . . and shimmer in the moonlight . . . we will go there one day . . . we'll ride on high . . . we'll sail through the sky . . . with a host of many."

"Amen, brother," somebody sang out.

"Where the colors are bright . . . yes, bright as the light that forms them in that rainbow . . . yeah . . . where grows a tree . . . a majestic tree . . . a tree which spreads her branches throughout the universe. And her fragrance . . . yes, Lord . . . her fragrance is sweet . . . yeah, sweet . . . y'all . . . as the plum ripened to blackness."

"Talk to us, Reverend!" a voice screamed out from the rear of the church, followed by Amens!

". . . And that fragrance, child, is filled with the
sweet smell of life. And that tree is full . . . tight . . .
bursting . . . with that life. But, I heard . . . yeah,
I heard . . . yeah, I heard one day that that old tree
was just standing there . . . yeah, strong . . . with those
arms stretched out wide across the land . . . when
the sky started to twisting and churning and the wind
started to racing and whistling and that old tree . . .
yeah, that tree . . . she held to her place . . . yeah . . .
tied to her roots . . . gathered all the strength she
had and stood fast . . . and she felt that wind circling
around her, and she felt her roots tearing from that
ground . . . yeah . . . she felt her roots pulling up
from that place. And that tree . . . yeah, that tree . . .
she lowered her mighty arms. She curved that mighty
trunk and bowed. She let that old wind pass over
her . . . yes, Lord, she let that old wind pass over.
Can you see it, Delia . . . can you see?"

Suddenly Madelia gasped. The seat below her floated away. She seemed to hover above it. Her daddy's voice was far away. She appeared to be in a chamber, hollow and distant. She could hear the voices of the people bouncing off some faraway wall.

"Yes, Daddy," she heard herself whisper, "I can see."

Madelia saw. She saw skies of vivid blues and greens. She saw streaks of gold shooting through a white

opening in the sky. The clouds were luminous and a rainbow parted to make room for a glistening chariot. Men, women, and children, dressed in robes of ice blue, stood with hands raised.

The chariot driver, in a purple gown, seemed to hover, open-winged, above his place at the front of the chariot. He lifted his arm to crack the long white feather whip. A multitude of horses in a multitude of colors charged forth, leaving a dust of pastel smoke.

Madelia rode that chariot through a storm, through
a funnel, past that tree, where she looked down
through that sky and saw her daddy's face. She saw
his eyes. She felt her heart.

Madelia's daddy raised himself and moved slowly backward, humming to the beat. Slowing the beat. Madelia's foot stopped, her heart slowed. She looked around the church. Arms were raised in praise. Heads bowed in prayer.

After the prayer, church was over. Sister Banks
helped Madelia and the other children to the rear of
the church. Everyone was shaking hands and hugging.
Madelia hugged her mama and shook hands with her
brothers and sisters. She saw her father shaking people's hands. His eyes searched the crowd and landed
on hers. He smiled. She smiled back.

On the way home the other children were talking, but Madelia wasn't listening. She was daydreaming about colors, beautiful colors. She remembered her jars of paint, and most of all, she remembered the sermon. She wouldn't need to copy her daddy's Bible.